The Bradford Family Adventures

Mystery at the Ballpark

by

Jerry B. Jenkins

MOODY PRESS
CHICAGO

Moody Press Edition 1990

Original title: *Mystery at Raider Stadium*

ISBN: 0-8024-0811-7

1 2 3 4 5 6 Printing/LC/Year 94 93 92 91 90

Printed in the United States of America

To Dan Ewald

Contents

1

Raider Stadium

Somehow in all of his nearly twelve years on earth, Daniel had never seen a Big League game in person.

He had liked Buck Spangler, the all star center fielder of the Richland Raiders, for as long as he could remember. He knew the batting averages of every Raider. He knew the averages of most every other hitter in the National League.

But Richland was four hundred miles from home. Dad and his big brother, Jim, had told him a lot about Raider Stadium and the two or three games they'd seen there. But this trip with his Sunday school department was Daniel's first.

The fourth-, fifth-, and sixth-grade boys from First Church followed their sponsor, Kenny Kaufman, up the steps from the dark hallways beneath the stadium. The big ballpark came into view. After the sky and the scoreboard in center field, the natural green grass was the first thing Daniel saw.

It was breathtaking. Daniel had tried to imagine it, but this was so much bigger. It was so much greener than he could have dreamed. He knew some of the other guys were talking to him, but it was as if he were in a daze.

He couldn't hear anyone or anything. And he certainly wasn't in a mood to talk. He had listened to games on the radio and watched them on television for his whole life. And now he just wanted to drink this in.

Kenny had promised the boys they would be there in time to see the teams, the Raiders and the Chicago Cubs, take batting practice. But to do that, they had to leave the church parking lot at four o'clock in the morning.

Most of the guys slept for the first couple of hours on the interstate highway. But Daniel was too excited. Mrs. Kaufman had been sick in the night and couldn't come along, Kenny said, so the boys would have to be especially good and obedient for him.

At around noon, Kenny had wheeled the bus into a parking lot. He ordered hamburgers for all eighteen boys. By then they were just an hour or so from the stadium. The boys were almost too excited.

Kenny had to make them quiet down and pick up all their garbage. Then he made buddy assignments. Each one had to keep track of one other guy so that someone would know where everybody was at all times.

"Who's gonna be your buddy, Mr. Kaufman?" someone yelled, and everyone laughed.

The boys had finally located their seats at the ballpark. Kenny told them that they couldn't go to the concession stands. The vendors would come around with food and drinks anyway. "And I couldn't keep track of you all." When anyone needed to go to the bathroom, Kenny insisted that two sets of buddies went—four boys in all.

Daniel carried his glove, the game program, and a magazine with pictures of the Raiders he hoped to get autographed. He sat staring as the Raiders practiced. He hadn't expected to see little movable fences here and there all over the field. He'd never seen that on television.

It was obvious what they were there for. All twenty-five Raiders were on the field while batting practice was going on. They were jogging, shagging flies, playing catch, and practicing their fielding. If it weren't for those little fences on wheels everywhere, all the players would have to watch every pitch and every swing to make sure the ball wasn't coming toward them.

In the outfield, one of the coaches was hitting high fly balls. Kenny said the long, skinny bat he was using was called a "fun go." In the infield, there were a couple of players at each position. They took turns catching anything hit their way by the practice hitters.

Even the batting practice pitcher threw from behind a short screen to protect him from line drives up the middle.

In the stands, the vendors had already begun selling soft drinks, beer, popcorn, peanuts, souvenirs, hotdogs, and ice cream. Daniel hated the smell of the beer, but all the other odors of the stadium mixed with the tobacco aroma to create a fragrance that was special.

Most of the other boys didn't seem as interested in what was happening on the field as they were about what was happening in the stands. Daniel couldn't understand that. He had hardly turned his eyes from the field since he'd sat down.

The Cubs came out of their dugout for batting practice, and the Raiders began to leave the field. Daniel wanted to run down to the front row and see if he could get some autographs. Several of his friends did. But Kenny Kaufman asked Daniel and his buddy, Chad Whiteford, to stay behind.

"I want to talk to you, Dan," Mr. Kaufman said. "Maybe you can get some autographs later. If not, I'll buy you a pack of the autographed pictures, OK?"

Daniel was disappointed, yet he was really a little nervous about asking for autographs anyway. And he had always wanted a set of the photos.

"I'm going to need your help today," Mr. Kaufman explained. "I can see already that even with the buddy system, there's no way I can keep track of everyone. Would you help me? Could I assign you three other sets of buddies besides yourself and Chad?"

"I guess so. What do I have to do?"

"Just keep an eye on them. Make sure they behave. Most of all, I want to know where they are. And most of the time, I'll want them right here in their seats. You're one of the older ones, and the other boys look up to you, Dan. Is it a deal?"

"Sure."

Daniel liked doing things for Kenny Kaufman. Kenny was a high school teacher. He was a tall, athletic man in his late twenties with sandy brown hair. He was the best hitter on the church softball team and the high scorer on the church basketball team.

He had a good sense of humor. He really seemed to enjoy the boys, and he especially liked Daniel. Maybe that was because Daniel was on the older end of the age group. Or maybe it was because he, too, was a sports fan. Regardless, Daniel would have done anything for Mr. Kaufman.

To Daniel, Kenny seemed a little worried that day. He figured it was because he had so many kids to watch without even his wife there to help. Eight of the kids sat in one row, including Daniel, Chad Whiteford, and the three other pairs of buddies for whom Daniel was responsible.

Behind them sat five more pairs of buddies and Mr. Kaufman. He carefully watched all the boys as they made their way down to near the home dugout. There they joined the mass of other boys and girls leaning over the rail and screaming for autographs.

Daniel watched, too. He was proud and honored that Mr. Kaufman would ask his help. But he was a little disappointed that he wasn't getting autographs. One thing made him feel better, though. Buck Spangler, his favorite player, was nowhere in sight.

A lot of the kids were chanting for him to come out, but he never did. When the others arrived back at their seats, Daniel said, "Guess we'll have to try to see Spangler after the game."

"Nah," one of the others said. "The other players say he never signs autographs. What a mean guy."

Daniel wanted to defend his favorite player. Maybe his teammates were just jealous. Maybe they felt bad that the kids were all asking for Buck. And maybe he really didn't have time to sign autographs. What if some kids saw him signing? He'd never be able to sign for everybody in the stadium. And Daniel knew everybody would want his autograph.

Spangler was in a slump, sure. But so were most of the Raiders. Still, they were only a game out of first place. The Mets and the Cubs were tied for first, as usual. So, if the Raiders won today, they would switch places with the Cubs. If the Mets happened to lose their game to the Cardinals, the Raiders would move into first place.

With just six weeks left in the season, the Raiders needed to make their move now and start hitting. Daniel just knew they could win the Eastern Division championship and beat the Atlanta Braves for the National League pennant.

Nobody else thought any team in the East could beat Atlanta. The Braves already led the Western Division by twelve games. They had beaten the Raiders four out of six times already. But Daniel noticed that when each team's best pitchers faced each other the Raiders won. And in a league championship series, it would be best against best.

Who would the Raiders, or whoever the National League champs were, face in the World Series? Daniel could only guess. Both races in the American League were close. But Daniel was picking the California Angels in the West and the Toronto Blue Jays in the East. He was hoping for a Raiders/Blues Jays world series.

Finally, both teams cleared the field. The grounds crew came out. That was something else Daniel had never seen on television. Did it ever look fun. They folded up the movable backstops and rolled them out to center field. There they stored them behind the wall.

A man on a little tractor dragged a wire mesh across the

infield. Two others drew the chalk lines up and down the first and third baselines. Another crew tidied up the pitcher's mound and cleaned off the rubber.

A couple of guys were using a wood frame to make the batter's box. Another man was painting home plate. A small crew hosed down the dirt part of the infield to settle the dust. When everything was ready, a local dignitary threw out the first ball. The four umpires met at home plate with the two managers. And a high school band played the national anthem while about half the people sang.

By game time, the stadium looked full to Daniel. The rest of the guys had settled down. And he was ready for a great game. He thought they might be in a good spot to catch a foul ball, so his glove was tight on his left hand.

Daniel was among the first to leap to his feet when Buck Spangler led the Raiders' charge from the dugout. They took the field in the top of the first. He was still standing when the starting pitcher was ready to begin the game. "Daniel," Chad Whiteford called, tugging at his sleeve. "I have to go the bathroom. Right now."

But Daniel wasn't listening.

2

Chad's Dad

It took little Chad Whiteford—a barely nine-year-old fourth grader with short, curly, dark hair—at least a half dozen tries to get anyone's attention. And when he got it, it wasn't Daniel's.

The first pitch of the game was a fastball that nearly hit the Cub batter. The crowd sat down. Kenny Kaufman leaned forward and grasped Daniel with a hand on each shoulder. "Better take Chad to the bathroom," he said. "Go to the one that's just to the left of the stairs behind us. If you're not back in five minutes, I'll come looking for you."

"But, Mr. Kaufman! The game just started!"

"C'mon, Dan. He can't wait, and you don't want to be out of your seat when the Raiders come to bat. I'll tell you if the Cubs do anything interesting while you go out with him."

Daniel talked Kenny out of making him take another pair with him. "I know where it is. And we'll be right back. No sense in making anyone else miss part of the game."

He followed the wiry, little fellow out to the aisle and down the steps. Daniel realized how wise Mr. Kaufman had been to put them together as buddies.

Chad had always looked up to Daniel, almost as much as Daniel looked up to Mr. Kaufman. Daniel was one of the best Bible verse memorizers in the church. And of course one of the best athletes for his age, too.

Chad always said "hi" to Daniel when he saw him in Sunday school or church. Daniel never really spent much time with the boy, but he thought he was cute. Daniel liked the fact that someone thought he was special. And he couldn't deny he tried to act better when he knew Chad was watching.

"Sorry I didn't go before," Chad said, turning around.

Daniel wanted to tell him, "Yeah, you should have thought of this before the game started. We've been here almost two hours."

But he didn't. He didn't want to hurt Chad's feelings. Anyway, he remembered when he was a little kid, really little, like first grade. His father had taken him to a high school football game where the only bathrooms were about a quarter of a mile from the stands.

Daniel had made his father take him at least three times. And though he didn't know it then, he found out later that it was always during the most exciting parts of the game. Remembering that, and hearing the crowd roar over what Daniel knew had to be the first Cub out, he simply said, "It's all right, Chad. Just hurry, huh?"

Chad handed Daniel his ball glove as the entered the huge public washroom. Daniel stood there, waiting with two gloves. He wondered what his own brother and sister, Maryann, felt like when they had to wait for him like this. He knew Chad didn't have an older brother. All he had was a three-year-old sister and a mother who made sure he got to all the church activities. Everyone felt sorry for Mrs. Whiteford. Her husband had left her soon after the little girl, Marie, was born.

"Does he ever write or call?" Daniel asked once, months before.

Chad nodded. "Every once in a while. Not often. He sends me lots of neat stuff. But it makes me feel kind of funny. I like playing with it and everything, but I don't want stuff. I want him. Only I guess he thinks the stuff will make me happy."

"But it doesn't?"

Chad shook his head.

Daniel had thought about that conversation many times over the past several months. He wanted to ask Chad more. But he wasn't sure he should. He wondered if his dad ever came to see him. He wondered if he ever talked about coming back, or anything like that.

Daniel decided that he shouldn't ask Chad such questions unless Chad brought up the subject.

They were heading back toward their seats when they heard a gigantic roar. They started running to find out what had happened. In the confusion, Daniel forgot to give Chad's glove back. He wound up sitting down with both.

"If you miss a foul ball, it sure won't be your fault," Kenny Kaufman teased. Many of the guys looked at Daniel with a glove on each hand and laughed.

"So, what happened?" Daniel asked, handing Chad his glove.

Everyone started talking at once. But finally Mr. Kaufman could be heard. "Cubs loaded the bases with one out. Then they tried to surprise the Raiders by bunting. The runner on third was sliding across the plate when the pitcher fielded the bunt. He fired to second and back to first for the double play."

"So they only scored one run?" Chad asked.

"No," Daniel said. "The run doesn't count because the double play ended the inning. But I'll bet somebody missed the bunt sign."

"Your're right," Kenny said. "Can you guess who?"

"Had to be the runner at first. He should have made it to second easily."

"Right. The catcher saw that he hadn't gotten a good

start. And he hollered at the pitcher to throw to second."

"Really?" Daniel said. "You'd think with the guy squaring around to bunt and the man charging in from third, the catcher wouldn't have even thought of that."

"Exactly," Kenny said. "Boy, you know your baseball. But the runner was sliding across the plate. I guess the catcher knew there was no way of getting him. So he looked up to see what the second best option was."

"And it turned out to be the best."

"Yeah, Dan. When you think about it, if the runner on third had been slow, they probably would have only gotten the out at home. They still would have had the bases loaded with the sixth hitter up. Let's see what he does in the second inning. We'll find out how important that double play was."

Most of the church kids had turned and were listening to Mr. Kaufman. They knew he knew his baseball. And they wanted to learn. "But it'll be a totally different situation," Ronnie Hanks said, pushing his glasses up higher on his nose.

"Right, Ronnie," Mr. Kaufman said. "Tell us in what ways the hitter might be batting differently."

"Well, there won't be any outs. Or any one on base. If he gets his pitch, he might be going for a homer. With the bases loaded and two outs, he would have been shortening up on the bat a little, and just trying to hit it anywhere."

"Good thinking. Still, if he gets good wood on the ball in the second inning, we can be glad for the double play."

Ronnie threw his head back and laughed. "I don't care if he strikes out. I thought the double play was great anyway!"

The Raiders were three up and three down in their half of the first. Daniel decided that he'd rather have taken Chad to the bathroom in the Raider half of the inning than the Cub half. Then Chad surprised him. He started talking again.

"My dad sure was glad to hear I was coming to this game."

"Really? You talked to him?"

"Yeah. Last week. Said he wished he could be here with me."

"Does he live around here?"

"No! He lives in Chicago. So even if he did come, he'd be rooting for the Cubs."

"Would he mind your rooting for the Raiders?"

"I wouldn't!"

Daniel was shocked. "You're a Cub fan? What a traitor! I ought to tell the other guys." But Daniel was smiling to show Chad he was just kidding.

"I'm not a Cub fan at all," the little guy explained. "But I wouldn't want to make my dad mad."

"Would he really be mad if you cheered for your favorite team?"

"I wouldn't want to find out. He can get kind of angry when things don't work out the way he wants them to."

Daniel wanted to ask, "Like what?" but he decided not to. If Chad wanted to talk about it, he would. It wasn't that Daniel wasn't curious. But the last thing he wanted to do was to make Chad feel bad.

The sixth hitter in the Cub's lineup popped out to second. That caused all sorts of buzzing among the church kids. Ronnie insisted that if he'd been hitting with men on and two outs, he wouldn't have been swinging so freely. Likely he would have driven in at least one run.

It was two out in the top of the second. The Cub pitcher hit a long, high home run to the opposite field that looked foul all the way. At least to everyone in the Raider dugout, the right fielder, and the manager.

But both the home plate and the first base umpires ruled it fair and a home run. Daniel jumped up and screamed with everyone else. He had a good view of the flight of the ball and knew it was a good call. He even persuaded his friends to admit it.

But the Raider manager and right fielder nearly got kicked out of the game for arguing. Buck Spangler just stayed in center field, keeping out of trouble.

During the time the Raiders were coming to bat, Chad wanted to talk again. "My dad doesn't like it very much that he doesn't get to see me."

"He doesn't get to see you?"

"Well, he used to. But one time he forgot to take me back home after a weekend. And Mom got him in trouble for it."

"He forgot!?"

"Yeah, well, sort of. He told me he would take me back Tuesday. And I said it was all right with me because I didn't want to go straight back to school anyway. He promised we could go to this big museum in Chicago."

"The Museum of Science and Industry?"

"No, the other one, Field something."

"Natural History."

"Yeah. And we went, and it was neat. But Dad forgot to call Mom, and she was real angry with him. I kept telling her that he just forgot, and that she shouldn't be so mad. But she said I didn't understand."

"So what happened?"

"She told somebody, and now Dad can only see me at our house. Which is bad."

"Why?"

"Because Mom has to be there. And they don't get along, and, and—"

"Oh. They fight and argue?"

"No. They try not to in front of me. But, you know, it's all quiet and embarrassing and everything. Dad keeps asking Mom if he can take me out for ice cream or something. And she says no, not unless she goes with me. Then he asks me if I want to go. And I say no, because she wouldn't let me have much ice cream anyway."

Daniel couldn't imagine a worse situation. He was so happy to have happily married parents.

3

Visit from a Stranger

Buck Spangler, the power hitting center fielder for the Raiders, hit a foul ball all the way out of the stadium on the first pitch leading off in the bottom of the second. He slammed his bat to the ground, and it broke in his hands.

Daniel and the other guys thought those two show of strength were pretty neat, but Daniel wondered why Buck was so mad. A few pitches later he lined to the first baseman, and though the Raiders put two men on with a walk and an outless fielder's choice, they failed to score again.

"Daniel, do you like me?" Chad Whiteford asked.

Daniel was surprised. "Well uh, sure, yeah, I like you. Why?"

"Just wonderin'."

"Why?"

"I don't know."

"Why wouldn't I like you, Chad? You're a good guy."

Chad shrugged as if he didn't want to talk about it anymore. The next time he spoke he was talking about his father again. "He says if I came to live with him, I could have a pony."

"In Chicago? Where would you ride it?"

"He said something about leaving it out on some farm. But that it would still be mine, and I could ride it whenever I wanted. You know my mom likes my dad, but he doesn't like her?"

Daniel looked into Chad's eyes. "How do you know that?"

"Just because my mom never says anything bad about him. She gets mad at him. But she gets mad at me, too, and she still likes me. She argues with him. And she makes sure he can't see me without her there. But she never says anything bad to me about him. She didn't look happy when I told her about the pony and living with him. I heard her arguing with him on the phone about it, but I do think she still likes him. At least most of the time I think she does like him."

"But he doesn't like her?"

Chad shook his head. "Huh-uh. Whenever he gets the chance, he asks me if she spanks me too much or too hard. Or if she hollers at me or is mean to me."

"And is she?"

"No way."

"So you tell him that?"

"No, I don't. I don't want to talk to him about her. Sure she spanks me and yells at me once in a while. But if I make a big deal out of it, maybe he'll make me stay with him."

"And you don't want to do that?"

"Not even for a pony."

"Why not?"

"Because he doesn't like my mom, and I do. He makes me feel bad when he says things about her all the time."

"Does he still do that?"

"He can't. Now he can only see me at our house and only once a month. But when I used to spend weekends with him, he would ask me all kinds of questions. And then he'd tell me how mean she had been to him. I think he was lying."

"Why?"

"Because I know my mom better than he does. She always trys to be fair, even with him. Even when he doesn't deserve it."

"What does he say about her?"

"He says she tries to keep him from seeing me. And that she kicked him out of the house. He says she wanted the divorce, and he didn't. And that she made up lies about him to get rid of him. I don't remember too much about it. But I know better than that."

Daniel wanted to know how Chad knew better. But again he felt he should wait and let Chad tell him.

The Cubs scored another run in the top of the third on back to back doubles. When the Raiders failed to reach base in the bottom of the inning, Daniel realized the Cub pitcher hadn't allowed a hit yet.

Behind Daniel, Kenny Kaufman stood and moved toward the aisle. "Taking a few of the guys for a bathroom break, Dan," he called back. "Make sure all of yours and the rest of mine stay right here."

Daniel nodded.

Not two minutes after Mr. Kaufman left, a man in a business suit approached the remaining boys. "You kids are all together here, right?" he asked.

They nodded.

"Scout troop? Little League team?"

"Nope," Ronnie said. "Sunday school department."

"How nice. Welcome to Raider Stadium. Who's here with you?"

"Mr. Kaufman," Daniel said. "I'm helping him."

"Just one man?"

"His wife got sick last night. Couldn't join us."

"Big job for one man," he said. "Bet you're a big help to him."

Daniel smiled.

"Have a good day and keep rooting for us," the man said, striding away.

The boys waved and smiled, asking each other who they

thought he was. "Bet he was the general manager," one said.

"No," said another, "I've seen pictures of the general manager. That wasn't him. I'll bet he's in charge of security or something."

The boys lost interest in figuring out who the man was. The Cubs staged another threat in the top of the fourth. The Raider starter walked the first two men on eight straight pitches. Then he fell behind the next hitter two and oh. The manager visited the mound. When the pitcher threw another ball, two relief pitchers started throwing in the Raider bull pen.

The Cub hitter was content to wait for his walk. But he took two straight fastballs right down the middle and hoped for one more he could smash out of the park. When it came, he was ready. His drive sent Buck Spangler and the left fielder toward the warning track in deep left center. The runners at first and second both tagged up, figuring the ball would be caught.

The left fielder waved Spangler off the ball and camped under it. But Buck brushed past him. He jostled the ball loose at the last instant. It hit the wall and bounced into Spangler's hands. The runners took off.

With his famous arm, Spangler rifled the ball all the way to the catcher. That forced the man rounding third to scamper back to the bag. A great cheer rose up from the crowd for the fabulous, run-saving throw. But Daniel, for one, realized that the ball should have been caught in the first place. Spangler, unless he had called for the ball—which, of course, Daniel couldn't know—had caused the mistake. His throw had saved the run, sure, but now it looked like he was scolding the rookie left fielder. Daniel had a bad feeling in the pit of his stomach. Maybe Buck Spangler wasn't all Daniel thought he was.

The Raider manager came out again, this time to switch pitchers. The starting pitcher was clearly upset. He dropped the ball on the mound before the catcher or even the manager could get there. He stomped off toward the dugout, trading shouts with the manager on his way by. Daniel realized he was seeing an awful lot more at the ball park than he ever saw on television. Maybe more than he wanted to.

Kenny Kaufman was none too thrilled that the boys had spoken to a stranger without finding out who he was. "Was he wearing a uniform, Daniel?"

"No."

"A badge? Identification of any kind?"

"No, but he welcomed us to the park and told us to keep rooting for the Raiders."

"Probably harmless," Kenny said, sighing. "But always try to get a name, Daniel."

"OK."

"Did he say anything else?"

"Not really."

"Did he ask you anything?"

"He asked for you, I think."

"By name? I don't think anyone knows we're here except the advance ticket office."

"No, he just asked who was here with us. Do you think anything's wrong with your wife, and they're trying to reach you?"

"Nah. They would just page me, I'm sure. What did you tell him?"

"I just told him your name, and that I was helping you."

Kenny looked troubled.

"Did I do the wrong thing, Mr. Kaufman? I didn't mean to. And he seemed like a nice enough guy, like an official or something."

"No, it's probably all right. It's just strange that he came by when I was gone, not while I was here."

"Maybe he'll come back when he sees you here," Daniel said.

"Maybe. What did he look like?"

"About forty or fifty, I guess."

"Forty or fifty? That's a big difference, Daniel. Gray hair?"

"No, all dark. No glasses. White shirt and tie, dark suit. Don't remember the color. Nice shoes."

"What do you mean by that?"

"Seemed real shiny and new, that's all."

"Anything else?"

"Not really. Should I be worried?"

Kenny shook his head. "No, don't let me scare you. I'll just stay close from now on. You learned a little lesson, right?"

Daniel nodded.

Chad sat quietly next to him, as if realizing that Daniel had just been corrected in a quiet way.

"You want to learn a little baseball lesson here, Dan?" Kenny Kaufman asked.

"Sure."

"Look at how the defense is playing with the bases loaded and no outs, and with a new pitcher in."

"They're playing back. Why? Don't they want to cut off the run at the plate?"

"Apparently not. They're only down by two. But they have to get out of this inning with as little damage as possible. If they play up to cut down the run and miss a double play opportunity, they may give up more than a run. They can't affort that."

A sharp ground ball to third saw the Raiders pull a third to second to first double play while a run scored. And when the next hitter flied out to center, Kenny Kaufman looked like a genius.

"You could be a Big League manager," Daniel said, smiling.

"No, I couldn't," Mr. Kaufman said. "I only told you what they were doing. The fact is, I would have played up to cut down the run. That grounder to third would have forced the runner at home. But it would not have resulted in a double play. Then that fly to center would have scored the run anyway. And they'd still be hitting with men on and two outs."

Daniel shook his head. He still thought Mr. Kaufman knew a lot about baseball. It made him feel even worse for having disappointed his teacher. He prayed that the man who had greeted them was just someone from the Raider front office. Maybe he would be back. Or maybe he would have the group greeted on the scoreboard or over the public address system.

Daniel hoped so.

4

The Greeting

Sure enough, after the Raiders saw a runner reach base on an error, in the bottom of the fourth, the scoreboard flashed a greeting to Daniel and his friends.

They didn't like the fact that the Raiders were down three to nothing and that they didn't even have a hit off the Cubs pitcher. Neither were they thrilled that the scoreboard welcomed them as "the junior high class at First Church."

But a greeting was a greeting. And, when they noticed it, they screamed and cheered. And the people around them clapped for them. Daniel wondered if maybe there was another group from another First Church somewhere that really was a junior high group. But there wasn't any cheering from any other part of the big ballpark. So Daniel and Mr. Kaufman—Daniel could tell by the look of relief on his face—felt certain that the stranger who had talked with them was someone from the Raiders. The message was a little mixed up. But still he had greeted them, and that was nice.

The Cubs threatened again in the top of the fifth. Their first batter hit a triple. He probably could have stretched it to an inside-the-park home run. But he was held up at third. And the Raiders pulled in their infield to protect against yet another run.

A ground ball to short was hit hard enough so the fielder could check the runner at third and still throw out the hitter without a run scoring. Then a sinking line drive was snatched off the left fielder's shoe tops. It was a play that so surprised and confused the runner at third that he had to dive back in to keep from getting picked off. Had he tried to tag and score, he'd have been out.

A weak tap right back to the mound accounted for the last out. The Raiders had held the Cubs scoreless for the first time since the first inning. Daniel was hoping the Raiders would at least get a hit in the bottom of the inning. Then they could concentrate on getting back some of those runs.

But now Chad was hungry. "My mother says I can't have regular soft drinks because of all the sugar," he told Daniel. "And the guys who are selling them in the stands don't have diet drinks. Can I go to the concession stand?"

"Can you wait until after the Raiders hit?"

"I'm really thirsty."

"Well, I want to see the Raider half of the inning. Spangler will be hitting fourth this inning if they can get somebody on. Anyway, I don't think Mr. Kaufman wants us going to the concession stand. You can ask him, though."

The Raider leadoff man crashed a double off the right center field wall. That gave the kids something to scream about, other than their scoreboard greeting. The Cubs didn't look any too worried. They were sitting on a three-run lead with their best pitcher on the mound.

But the no-hitter had been broken up. And it appeared Buck Spangler would get to hit in the inning with a least one runner on. Meanwhile, Chad Whiteford was begging Kenny Kaufman to let him go to the concession stand. He explained the whole thing about needing a diet drink so he wouldn't get so much sugar.

The next hitter was out on a weak roller to short. But the

runner on second advanced to third.

"Watch this," Kenny Kaufman told the boys. "I'll bet the Raider manager calls for a squeeze play."

"Really, Mr. Kaufman? Why?"

"Because the Cub pitcher is throwing so well. They may not get another hit off him till later in the game. They've got a guy on third and only one out. They need to start chipping away at this lead while they can. They'll sacrifice an out to get a run in. Then they'll be down by only two."

"What's a squeeze play?" Chad wanted to know.

Daniel explained. "That's where the batter bunts while the runner on third charges toward the plate. If the hitter gets the bat on the ball, there's no way the runner can be thrown out because he'll be across the plate by the time anyone fields it. It's risky, though, because when the pitcher sees the batter square around to bunt, he usually throws the ball high or close to him to make it harder to bunt. And if the batter tips the ball up in the air and someone catches it, the runner at third will be an easy out."

The Cubs had an idea what the Raiders might do, too. They pulled their first baseman in for the possible bunt.

"They should bring their third baseman in, too, shouldn't they?" Chad asked. "All the hitter has to do is bunt it toward him, and he'll be back too far to field it."

"He'll come running in with the pitch," Kenny said. "If he comes in too soon, it allows the runner to lead off halfway down the line. They have to hold him close. Or he'll get such a big jump he could steal home even if the batter doesn't get the bat on the ball."

The pitcher pitched from the stretch, rather than from a full windup, in an attempt to hold the runner close to the bag at third. In fact, before his first pitch to the plate, he tried to pick the runner off. It wasn't close. But the throw nearly got away from the third baseman, bringing the Raider crowd to its feet. That would have been the easiest way to score.

Mr. Kaufman was right. As soon as it was clear that the next throw was headed to the plate, the third baseman charged up the line. The batter took a full swing. The first and third basemen weren't more than thirty feet from him. The line drive whistled past the first baseman foul down the right field line. On the next pitch, the infielders didn't charge in so fast.

The ball was bunted about ten feet straight up in the air and directly in front of the plate. The pitcher raced in. The catcher leaped out toward the ball. He hoped to catch it and double the runner off third to kill the inning.

The third base coach screamed at the flying runner to get back. But he was almost to the plate already. He planted his feet to stop and turn back. But the ball hit the pitcher's glove and rolled to the catcher.

The runner saw that the ball had not been caught. He knew he had a better chance to score than to get back to third. So he changed directions again and dove for the plate. Unfortunately, the catcher was diving for the same place, and the tag beat the runner. Two outs, man on first, Raiders still down by three.

"They've got to get the man into scoring position," Kenny said.

"Which means what?" Chad asked.

Ronnie Hanks answered. "Second base, so he can score on a single. Maybe."

On the first pitch to Buck Spangler, the runner took off. He had a good jump on the pitch. He would have stolen second easily, but Spangler was trying to catch the Cubs napping. He squared around as if to bunt, obviously just to confuse them. But the pitch sailed in on him, and he had to dance to get out of the way. The ball nicked his bat, was ruled a foul ball, of course, and the runner had to go back to first.

Would they send him again? No one knew.

"Time for the hit and run," Kenny said. "The runner goes, and Spangler tried to hit it behind him."

"Everybody runs after they hit the ball, don't they?" Chad asked.

"Yes. But on a hit and run, the runner starts going, and then the hitter tries to hit the ball to right field. So the runner can at least get to third."

"Then why don't they call it the run and hit?" Chad asked.

Mr. Kaufman smiled. "Good question," he said. "Guess it just doesn't have the same ring to it."

Once again, the runner had second stolen. But he had to go back when Spangler fouled off the pitch. Two outs, two strikes, man on first. The runner took off yet again, and, this time, Spangler came through. The pitcher had tried to keep the ball inside, making it harder to hit to right. But Buck stepped away and swung a little late, driving the ball deep into right field.

By the time the right fielder caught up with it, it was bouncing around in the corner. And Spangler was flying around second. The run scored, and only a good relay from the first baseman kept Spangler at third. The next hitter struck out. But the Raiders had picked up a run.

"Should have been at least two," Kenny said.

Daniel was worried. The Cubs' heavy hitters were due up. And middle relief was the weakest part of the pitching staff.

"Now can I go get a diet drink?" Chad asked.

5
The Page

It was the top of the sixth inning. Thousands were milling about beneath the stands, waiting in line for food or souvenirs and heading for the washrooms.

Kenny Kaufman had decided to stay behind with the other boys while Daniel took Chad Whiteford to the concession stand. "You're not going to just get a diet drink after we wait here forever, are you?" Daniel asked.

"No, I guess I'll get a hot dog, too. Maybe some chips."

That made Daniel hungry. He checked his wallet. He had more than enough for a lot more food, some souvenirs, and even an emergency, should one arise. But he had promised his mother he wouldn't buy a bunch of junk or eat too unwisely.

"I know you'll eat too much at the ball game like your father and your brother always do," she had told him the night before. "But try not to make yourself sick."

He decided that another hot dog, some caramel corn, and a large drink would tide him over until dinner on the way home. He smiled. He imagined his mother shaking her head as he ate twice as much as he would have at home. He would get a team photo and maybe a batting glove, too. But that would have to wait until later.

Chad didn't seem in the mood to talk about his family anymore. And even though Daniel was still curious, he was determined to leave it alone unless Chad brought up the matter again.

Daniel heard the screams of the crowd and wondered what had happened. If they were closer to the front of the hot dog line, he could have seen what happened on the television monitor. But his view was blocked.

The people kept cheering, and Daniel had a decision to make. He wondered if he could see what was going on by dashing up to the top of the concrete steps and looking onto the field. He knew shouldn't leave Chad in line alone. But he told himself he could still see him from the steps.

He looked at the line, which was moving slowly. It might be ten minutes before they got to the front. He looked toward the steps and knew that his other friends were sitting just a few feet away from there. Even if whatever had happened on the field was over by now, someone there might see him and tell him. Or he could call over to them. He couldn't run back to them because he would lose sight of Chad. But maybe, just maybe. . . .

He turned to Chad. "Listen, wait here and save my place, OK?"

Chad nodded uncertainly.

"It'll be all right, Chad. I just want to see what's happening. And I won't go farther than those stairs. OK?"

Chad nodded again, and Daniel walked over to the steps. When he reached the top, he could see the Cub manager and two coaches arguing with the home plate umpire. Fans all over the place were yelling, "Throw him out! Throw him out! Boo! Get him off the field!"

"What happened?" Daniel asked a boy nearby. He knew he could never get his friends to hear him from that far away.

"They thought the pitcher was throwing at their hitters. Probably was, too. But there was no call, no warning. This'll probably wind up being one of those games where each team starts throwing at everybody. Then there'll be a big brawl."

"Hope not," Daniel said, turning back toward the stairs.

"Hope so," the other boy said. "Exciting."

Daniel thought that was kind of sick. But he understood what the kid meant. It was interesting to see the arguing and a little fighting, because no one ever seemed to get hurt. But if two fastball pitchers started throwing at players on the other teams, that could really be dangerous. He'd hate to see Buck Spangler get hurt or thrown out for fighting if he almost got hit.

When he bounded back down the stairs to the line, he nearly panicked. He couldn't see Chad. Why had he taken his eyes off him? Where could he be? What would he tell Mr. Kaufman? And who would watch the other kids if Kenny had to help him find Chad? Maybe they could ask an usher to help.

Daniel ran from one end of the line to the other. For a second he thought he saw the man who had greeted them earlier. Maybe he could help by having Chad paged or something.

But Daniel lost sight of the man, and suddenly, right here in front of him, was Chad. "Chad! Where have you been? You scared me half to death!"

"I came looking for you. I'm sorry I lost our places in line, but you said you could see me from the top of the stairs. I figured if you could see me, I could see you. Only I couldn't see you, so I thought you couldn't see me. And I got kind of scared and came looking for you. You ran right past me, you know."

"Well, I thought you were still in line. Now next time stay where I tell you, OK?"

"OK. Daniel, are you mad at me?"

"No, I just don't want to lose you."

"That's nice."

"I didn't mean it to be nice. But stay put, would you? I

guess I shouldn't have left you here anyway. But there's no sense making it more dangerous than it needs to be. Mr. Kaufman already said he was going to come looking for us if we weren't back in a few minutes. Let's just go back, huh?"

"No, Daniel. I still want something to eat. I'm very hungry."

"We can get a hot dog when the vendors come around."

"But I can't get a diet drink."

"I'll buy you some ice cream. Two ice creams. OK?"

Chad thought for a moment. "Does ice cream have sugar in it?"

"Of course!"

"Then I can't have it. Makes me hyperactive."

"What?"

"C'mon, Daniel. We're in line. Let's just stay here."

Daniel shrugged and resigned himself to it. He knew Mr. Kaufman would come looking for them soon. And he hated to bother him. He knew Kenny wouldn't want to be gone from the others too long, so he kept watching the stairs where he might appear. He would just wave at Mr. Kaufman to assure him they were all right. Kenny wouldn't have to come all the way down.

While Daniel kept his eyes on the top of the stairs, Chad was talking to him. But Daniel wasn't concentrating. "Hm? What'd you say?"

"I said I saw that man again, the one who came and talked to you in the stands."

"Yeah," Daniel said absently, still looking elsewhere. "I thought I saw him, too. Where was he?"

"Over there."

Daniel looked to see where Chad was pointing. It wasn't the same place where he had seen the man. *The guy sure must get around,* Daniel thought. *He must be with the Raiders.*

When he turned back to look at the stairs, he realized they had hardly moved in the line. He wished Chad hadn't lost their place. At least thirty people must have gotten in ahead of them when Chad left the line.

And here came Kenny.

"Mr. Kaufman!" Daniel yelled. "We're right here! Just stuck in a long line! We'll be right up! Need anything?"

Kenny just smiled and waved and shook his head. Then, as if reconsidering, he called back. "Yeah! Bring me a snack! Anything! Surprise me."

"What's happening in the game?" Daniel asked.

"Lots of Cubs have been thrown out! A hitter, the manager, and a coach! It's gonna get interesting! Hurry back! Two outs!"

Daniel just hoped the Cubs wouldn't start throwing at the Raiders now. On the other hand, if they could get that pitcher thrown out, that would be better for the Raiders in the long run. The man had allowed only one run on two hits all day.

By the time Daniel and Chad got to the front of the line, it was obvious the Raiders were batting again. And that there was something exciting going on. Daniel was eager to get back to find out. He was tempted to let Chad pay for the stuff and carry it all back to where they were sitting. But he knew he'd get into big trouble for that. They bought their hot dogs and their chips and their drinks—a diet one for hyperactive Chad—and a treat for Mr. Kaufman.

And then Daniel heard a familiar name over the public address system.

"Paging Mr. Kenneth Kaufman. Mr. Kenneth Kaufman, please. Come to the customer relations office."

6
The Disappearance

Now Daniel was really confused. What could the page mean? Who knew Mr. Kaufman was even at the game? Well, all the parents knew, of course. And the pastor. And Mr. Kaufman's wife.

Maybe something was wrong with his wife. Why else would he be called to the office? For a phone call? Of course. What else?

Daniel wondered if Mr. Kaufman had heard the page. He hadn't remembered being able to hear much of anything from inside the ballpark. Down below the stands, where the public address system echoed off the concrete walls, it was easy to hear.

The call for Mr. Kaufman came again. Daniel assumed it was more urgent this time. He didn't know why. Maybe it was because he was sure Kenny couldn't have heard it. He hurried through the crowd toward the stairs. The place seemed more crowded than ever, especially when he didn't have a hand free to keep his balance.

He called over his shoulder for Chad to stay close behind. When he saw a little opening, he hurried. As he reached the bright sunlight, he squinted against the glare, searching the area where his friends should have been. He saw a bunch of them. But he didn't see Mr. Kaufman.

Had he already heard the page? And was he trying to get to the customer relations office? Or was he waiting for Daniel to get back before leaving the rest of the kids?

Just then the Raider catcher, hitting in the bottom of the sixth, was hit in the head with a pitch. The crowd went crazy as both dugouts emptied. Players from each team were wrestling and rolling around on the field.

Just as the umpires seemed to be restoring peace and order, another fistfight erupted. And the teams were at it again.

"Daniel!" Kenny shouted. "Where have you been?"

"Looking for you! Did you hear the page?"

"Yes! Can you keep track of the guys for a while? I don't know if there's a phone call or what. So I don't know how long I'll be. Don't let anyone go anywhere, hear?"

"OK."

As Daniel moved past him, Mr. Kaufman clapped him on the shoulder as if to thank him and encourage him that he knew Daniel could handle it. And he said, "Is Chad with you?"

"Yeah," Daniel said, nodding behind him.

"I don't see him," Mr. Kaufman said, not sounding worried yet.

Daniel's heart sank, He spun around. "He was just here. Right behind me."

"He isn't now. You'd better find him quick. Tell the other guys to sit still. He can't be far. I'll keep an eye out for him, too, between here and the concession stand. If you don't find him, have an usher page him. And have him head for the customer relations office, OK?"

Daniel nodded and took his food to the rest of the guys. He didn't even have time to tell them it was not for them. They jumped in and started sharing everything. "I'm going back to look for Chad!" he shouted.

They ate and watched the end of the brawl and generally ignored him.

"Nobody is allowed to leave here for any reason until Mr. Kaufman or I get back, OK?" No one responded. "OK?" he repeated, louder.

"Awright," Ronnie muttered. "I'll tell'em, Dan."

"Thanks."

Order had finally been restored on the field. Players were ejected and warnings given. Now a pinch hitter for the Raider pitcher stood in against the new reliever. Daniel knew he didn't have time to watch, even though the batter represented the tying run.

He slowly stepped down the top two stairs. But he whirled around when he heard the crack of the bat and sensed the crowd rising. He was too far down the steps to see the flight of the ball. As he reached the top again and jumped up and down, he saw both Raiders trotting around the bases. Home run. Tie game.

But until he could find Chad, the game, win or lose, made no difference. He wasn't really worried yet. Mostly he was mad at Chad. Couldn't he stay next to Daniel for a few minutes in a crowd? They had both been carrying stuff, but it wasn't that difficult.

He hadn't decided yet whether he would scold Chad. He simply wanted to find him and get back to the game. Daniel was more worried about what Mr. Kaufman's phone call—or whatever it was—was all about.

The thousands of people who had jammed the concession stands at the top of the sixth were surging toward their seats. The game was tied, and the Raiders were threatening to go ahead. Daniel couldn't stay. He knew that. Yet he knew something else, too. After a home run, the pitcher will often take out his anger by brushing back the next hitter.

In a game like this one, that wouldn't be too smart. There had already been arguments and a fight and several players thrown out. Daniel debated staying at the top of the steps just for the first pitch to the next hitter. But he knew he couldn't.

He didn't know if Chad had slipped by him and was already sitting with the guys again or what. He turned to look up the stairs and heard an unbelievable roar again. It was just as he had suspected. The pitch had not hit the Raider hitter, but it had brought the teams out onto the field again.

Daniel didn't care much to see another fight. But he did hope the Raiders would be able to go ahead in the game. He shook his head as if to clear his mind. He knew he had only one important thing to worry about: Chad Whiteford.

He charged to the bottom of the stairs and through the crowd. He went all the way to the back of the long tunnel that went both ways around the stadium. If Chad had not gone up the stairs with the crowd—and wasn't in the bunch of people he had just come through—he had to have gone one way or the other through the dark corridors.

Daniel pressed his back up against the cool, concrete wall and looked to his right. Nothing. There were lots of kids, some with curly hair, but all with adults. There was one dark-haired man in a suit running toward Daniel. It might have been the man he had seen earlier. But he was running so hard and fast that Daniel couldn't tell.

The man's hair was flying. His tie had come loose from inside his vest and was slung over his shoulder. His suit jacket was flapping in the breeze, and his shoes were making a clackety racket in the hallway.

Daniel wanted to watch him but knew he had to check for Chad the other way. He looked to his left. There, at the end of the tunnel, near an exit that allowed sunlight in, was a man running and pulling a young boy behind him.

The man was moving so quickly that the boy's feet were hardly touching the ground. But he looked like Chad. He seemed to have curly hair, and, though Daniel couldn't make out the colors, he seemed to be dressed like Chad.

Daniel had only one choice. He had to follow. He started jogging that way, completely forgetting about the other man, the one running up behind him. By the time he felt the pounding footsteps, it was too late to move. The man blasted into him, slamming him up against the wall, banging his forehead, and leaving them both, sprawled and rolling, on the floor.

The man cursed and jumped to his feet. It was the same man, the one who had greeted the boys. Daniel just knew he had to be with the ball team. Maybe he was with security. Maybe he saw that someone was being kidnapped and was running to save him.

The man limped now but was still moving quickly. Daniel was dazed but ran to catch up with him. "I know that kid!" he shouted. "He's my friend. Catch that guy, catch him!"

The man looked back desperately and tried to speed up. Whatever it was he had injured in the fall was hurting him worse now. He couldn't speed up. He lurched along, trying to stay ahead of Daniel. He seemed to be trying to catch the man and the boy who was being dragged from the stadium.

Daniel nearly caught the man. He repeated his frantic plea that he catch the kidnapper. But the man slipped in some spilled food. Had Daniel taken the time to look at it, he would have known that it was the stuff he and Chad had bought just moments before. Whoever had kidnapped Chad had swept him off his feet from the middle of the crowd and pulled him away.

Daniel reached for the arm of the running man. "How can I help?" he yelled. "I'm pretty fast. But what do I do if I catch them?"

The man shoved him aside. Daniel ran into a little old woman and an usher who yelled at him and told him to quit running. But he couldn't quit. He was sure it was Chad now, more sure than he'd ever been of anything. He had to catch them. He had to help the Raider executive. It was obvious he was hurt and couldn't go much farther.

Daniel lit out after them again. He felt less dazed than

he had when he had hit the wall. He was stunned by having run into two more people. But from somewhere he got a second wind. He prayed as he ran that God would give him the strength he needed.

In less than a minute, he had caught the dark haired man again and grabbed his suit jacket from behind. The man stopped and faced him. "Look!" he shouted, pushing Daniel hard to the ground. "Buzz off! This is official business, and I'll handle it! I don't need any help from you!"

There was something in his look that Daniel didn't like. He didn't like being thrown to the ground again either. But he didn't know what it was that pulled him up and started him running again.

He was mad now. If that man was on official business and knew what he was doing, he should welcome any help he could get. What if the kidnapper lost him somehow? Wouldn't he want to know who Chad was? His description? What he was wearing?

It didn't make sense. Daniel didn't know exactly who he was facing, but he sure wasn't going to give up. He could only hope that the little boy wasn't being kidnapped.

What he didn't know was whether the chasing man was trying to stop the kidnapper or help him. Either way, Daniel had to find out. He had to help the man if he could. Or to save Chad from both of them.

7

The Chase

Daniel found himself running again, maybe faster than he had ever run before in his life. His breath came in short bursts. His fists were clenched, arms pumping with the effort.

He was overheating, he knew that. He wanted to shed his jacket, but he didn't want to take the time. In front of him the limping man was struggling along, trying to catch the man with the boy, the boy Daniel knew was his friend Chad. The strange thing was, Daniel listened for screams or cries from Chad, but all he heard was laughter. Surely that couldn't be from Chad!

They reached the end of the tunnel. The man dragged Chad through a doorway next to an overhead door huge enough for trucks to drive through.

Daniel couldn't figure out why the man didn't just go through the larger opening. Then he saw workers standing near it. Apparently they were there to keep people from coming and going through there.

Daniel was gaining on the limping man. He knew he would catch him soon. In fact, he would have a better chance of catching the kidnapper himself, if the man would just let him get by.

Daniel edged to the left so that he could see through the opening. He wanted to see where the man and Chad had gone. The door they burst through had shut behind them, and they hadn't turned left across the opening.

Through the big door, Daniel saw a van pulling away. A shiny, black station wagon was sliding into the parking place it had left. He caught the limping man just as he reached the doorway. "They pulled away in a van!" he shouted. "Are you going to follow them?"

The man glared at Daniel as he passed through the door. "Yeah, matter of fact I am."

"Can I go with you? I know the boy, and I can help you."

"Maybe you should," the man said. He grabbed Daniel's arm and guided him into the back seat of the station wagon. The man jumped in the passenger's side of the front seat. And the driver pulled away fast, making the tires screech.

"That's the van!" Daniel said, pointing to a vehicle about a block ahead.

The driver looked at the other man. "What's with *this* kid?"

"Friend of Chad's," he said. "Might be of use to us."

"How'd you know his name?" Daniel asked. "Who are you guys anyway?"

"Who did you think we were?" the injured man asked.

"I thought you were with the Raiders. I thought you saw a kid kidnapped, and you wanted to help."

"That's exactly right. I'm Phil, and this is Stan. We're in security." He flashed a badge. But Daniel didn't get a good look at it.

"How did you know they were going to get away in that van?"

"What do you mean?"

"I mean how did you know to have the car waiting right there?"

"I, uh, radioed ahead for Stan to meet me here when I

was chasing them. We were just lucky their getaway van was right here, too."

"You've got radios?"

"Yeah, here under the dashboard. See?"

"Wow. Shouldn't you get closer to the van?"

"We're close enough."

Stan, an older man, turned on the radio. It crackled, then a staticky message came: "You back there, Phil?"

Stan reached for the button on the transmitter and clicked it twice.

"Somethin's wrong with this," he said.

"No, there isn't," Daniel said. "Someone was calling you, Phil."

Neither man said anything, or even looked at Daniel. The radio crackled again: "What's two clicks s'posed to mean. You guys all right back there or what?"

Phil picked up the transmitter. "We're all right, Dwight," he said. "Just got a little company, that's all."

"Cops?"

"Nah. A kid. Friend of Chad's. Got a good look at me and the vehicles, so I thought we'd better bring him along."

Daniel nearly stopped breathing. The van ahead of them was no longer speeding. As they got closer he could see just what he suspected. There was a radio antenna on the van, too. These men were talking to Chad's kidnapper. They were all in on it together!

He wanted to shout at them. He wanted to tell them he had figured it out. But they knew that. He slumped back in the seat. The question now was, Why had they chosen Chad? They knew his name somehow. This Phil guy had obviously been checking on him when he greeted the kids earlier.

Daniel's heart pounded. He had no idea how many men there were in the van. He wanted to stay close to Chad to help him get free. But he knew he might have a better chance if he could get away and call the police.

He looked around the station wagon carefully. He memorized the colors and style. He memorized the license number of the van and its make and model. When both stopped in heavy traffic at a light, he bolted out of the back door. He sprinted down a side street as fast as he could.

As he was leaving the car, he heard Phil say, "Go after him, Stan. My leg will never make it."

Daniel knew he could outrun the old man. But when he looked back, he was surprised that the old guy moved pretty well. And he had a look of determination on his face. Daniel felt bad for trying to get away rather than staying with Chad. But he knew there was little the two of them could do against at least three adults.

"Stop that kid!" Stan shouted. "He stole my wallet!"

Several people grabbed for Daniel, slowing him down. "I did not!" he screamed. "He's trying to kidnap me!"

"A little thief, huh?" a woman said, emerging from a drugstore with a broom. She tossed it between Daniel's legs, causing him to tumble hard on the pavement. Several people cheered. Daniel wondered how God could let this happen to him.

His knees and ankles throbbed as he fought to jump up again. But the big man wrapped his arms around him and lifted him off the ground. Daniel kicked and screamed, "He's kidnapping me! He's a kidnapper!"

"Whip the little thief!" people shouted. "Yeah, give him a good beating!"

Daniel was frantic as Stan hustled him back to the station wagon. Cars behind them were honking. Phil had slid over to the driver's side. Just as Stan was piling Daniel into the front seat between them, Daniel's eyes caught those of a woman in a car behind them. "Help!" he bellowed as loud as he could. "Call the police."

He was so relieved when she shifted into park and leaped from her car. She stared at the license number and ran into a store as Phil pulled away. Daniel prayed that she would reach the police fast.

The voice of Dwight from the van came over the radio again, demanding to know what in the world was going on.

Phil explained, including the part about the lady who appeared to be calling the police.

"We don't need that," he said. "Think up a story to tell if you get stopped, and, if the kid doesn't go along with it, he'll never see Chad again."

Each of the men in the front seat had an elbow pinning Daniel back against the seat. "Did you get that, kid? If the cop stops us, I'm going to tell them a little story, and you're going to agree to it, all right?"

Daniel didn't answer.

"You know what's going to happen to your little friend if you don't cooperate?"

Still Daniel didn't answer. Phil looked as if he was ready to punch him. Stan spoke. "Whatever happens to Chad will be your fault, kid," he said. It's your choice. His only chance to how you do."

Within minutes, Daniel could hear the sirens. The woman had succeeded! The traffic was thick and barely moving, and people were clearing the way for the police. Two squad cars were coming from one direction and two from another. They wer using their loudspeakers to clear the way.

Daniel noticed the van pulling ahead to get out of the way, and it didn't wait. If only he could somehow tell the police about the man and the van! He would be safe, but what about Chad? Chad wouldn't have a chance. And it would be Daniel's fault.

As the police got closer to the car, they drew their guns. That shocked Daniel. Apparently they weren't taking any chances in case the woman who called had been right.

"Out of the car. Hands above your heads!"

Phil pasted on a big, charming smile as he emerged. "Don't make my brother get out, if you don't mind. Bad heart, you know. I know what this is all about—"

But the policemen grabbed him and turned him toward the car. They forced him to lean against the roof with his hands above his head. "Feet back and spread them," the police officer barked.

Another policeman pulled Stan from the car and searched him.

"I have a weapon," Phil said. "Left hip. Snub nosed thirty-eight. I'm a private investigator, fully licensed to carry it. Careful."

"Thank you, Mr. Schaefer," the policeman said, his tone changing somewhat as he studied Phil's license. He handed the pistol to his partner. "We received a report of a kidnapping that included a description of the boy in your car and your car. Also your brother. Apparently, his heart didn't bother him when he was chasing the kid and carrying him to the car."

Phil laughed. "Actually it did. And, if you'll let me explain, we can straighten this whole thing out. The boy is my son, Skip, and that's his uncle. We were all at the Raider ball game. But we had to leave early because Stan has to work tonight. He's a security guard.

"Well, the boy loves the Raiders. He's followed them all his life. He tried to get out of the car and run back to the stadium. His uncle chased him down, but it's all right now. That's all."

Phil was still smiling. Stan was nodding earnestly. Daniel still sat in the middle of the front seat. His heart was cracking against his ribs. He wanted to jump out, to shout, to scream, to get the police to follow the van.

But if the man in the van didn't hear from Phil and Stan soon, would he kill Chad? And whose fault would that be?

The policeman leaned in the car and smiled at Daniel. "Sorry about the trouble, Skip. Do you have any form of identification?"

"No. I'm only twelve."

"Can you just tell me then if what this man is telling me is true. Is he your father?"

8
The Decision

Daniel's eyes burned into the officer's. He wished against all hope that the expression on his face would say more than the words from his mouth. "Yes, sir. That's my dad. And I wanted to stay at the game because the Raiders were ahead after five innings. I'm sorry I caused all this trouble."

The officer studied him carefully. "That's all right," he said slowly. "I understand. These things happen. You behave yourself now, hear?"

"Yes, sir."

"Sorry for the trouble, Mr. Schaefer," the office said. "We have to check these things out, you know."

"Sure. Used to be a cop myself. Just doin' your job, I know. Thank you."

Phil let Stan drive again as they pulled back into traffic. "You did a good job, kid. You must value the life of your little friend."

"Course I do. Would the man in the van really kill him?"

"Are you kidding? Not a chance. The man in the van is Chad's father."

Daniel was totally confused. Why would a man kidnap

his own son? Maybe Chad *had* been laughing in the stadium. That's why he wasn't screaming for help! Maybe his father had just swept him off his feet, spilling his food and half carrying, half dragging him to the van. Daniel only wondered what Chad's father had promised him this time.

He turned to Phil, the one the policeman had called Mr. Schaefer. "So, you're not going to hurt Chad?"

"Nope. We were just paid to help put him back where he belongs. And where he wants to be."

"What do you mean? Who paid you?"

"His father, Dwight Whiteford."

"So why did you bring me along?"

"Because you were making a pest of yourself. And I was worried that you could describe me and the van and the car. That would slow us down, which you've already done a good job of."

Daniel felt glad, of course, that he had slowed them down. If only there was a way to do it again. "What happens to me now?"

"Nothing. When we get some distance between Chad and your Mr. Kaufman, his father's going to take him somewhere where no one will bother them. Away from the abusive mother and other people who would try to leave him there."

"Abusive mother," Daniel said. "I know his mother, and—"

"If you know his mother, you know she's mean to him. He wants to live with his father. And it's dangerous for him to stay where he is. He's been telling his father for a long time that he wants out, and that he wants to live with him. But Dwight just can't get all the legal problems straightened out."

"I don't believe that."

"It doesn't make much difference what you believe, kid. I believe it. And that's why I'm helping him."

"Helping him break the law? That's what you're getting paid for?"

"Sometimes you have to do what's right, even if it's against the law."

"Have you ever talked to Chad about it?"

"No, but I've known his father for many years. I know he would never lie."

Daniel knew better, of course, because of all the things Chad had told him. "What were you doing talking to us at the ball game like you were someone with the Raiders or something?"

"Just trying to see what the layout was like. We thought there was going to be just a young husband and wife watching nearly twenty kids. We couldn't believe our luck when it was just one guy with all you boys. I knew eventually we'd get you separated from him, and we'd get our chance."

"But who had the greeting put up on the scoreboard?"

Phil smiled. "I did. All part of the game. I told the customer relations office that I was Mr. Kaufman and had a bunch of boys here."

"What about the call Mr. Kaufman got when I was in line with Chad at the concession stand?"

"Mine, too. You told me his wife was sick, so—"

"I told you?"

"Sure. Don't you remember? You were a friendly little guy. Very helpful. Until now. Now you're in the way."

Daniel wanted to kick himself. How could he have been so foolish to tell a stranger information like that? Everything he had said, the man had used against Chad and Mr. Kaufman, and now Daniel himself.

Yet the man had seemed so nice and friendly. He was charming. He smiled a lot. He looked like an official. He acted like someone from the ball club. Daniel decided that he had learned a big lesson the hardest way possible.

At least he was glad that this wasn't a real kidnapper. He knew Phil Schaefer was not the type of a man who would hold a kid and demand money from his parents before giving him back.

But he was still a liar and a lawbreaker. And he wasn't

too smart if he believed everything Mr. Whiteford told him about Mrs. Whiteford and Chad.

"Anyway," Phil Schaefer continued, "you told me his wife was sick, so I thought it would make sense to him if he got a call to the phone during the game."

"So what happened when he got to the office?"

"Nothing. I had him paged. But I wasn't there when he got there. You and Chad had stood so long in the concession line that I figured he'd come looking for you. So it was the perfect time to have him called away. When the page turned out to be phony, he'd be more worried about getting back to the rest of the kids than about worrying where you and Chad were. At least for a while. My job was to buy time and then to see which of us had the best chance at grabbing Chad. As it turned out, Chad got separated from you, I guess. The next thing I knew Dwight was on his way out with him."

Daniel realized then that Phil Schaefer didn't know that Mr. Kaufman knew Daniel and Chad had gotten separated. Daniel knew that the first thing Mr. Kaufman would do when he found out that there was no message would be to call his wife and then the church. Then he would probably get someone in the customer relations office to describe the man who left the message.

When he realized it was the same man who had talked to the boys, he would probably race back to them. He would discover that Daniel and Chad still had not returned. He would get an usher or security people to watch the rest of the boys. Mr. Kaufman would start searching for Daniel and Chad.

That, Daniel knew, would let Kenny Kaufman know quickly that they were not still in the stadium. Once word got out that Daniel and Chad were missing—and that a certain man was suspected—the local police departments would be notified.

Daniel prayed that the policeman who had talked to them would remember his description. They already had

Phil Schaefer's name and address. They had the kind of car he was driving. But they had nothing on the van yet.

"Where are we going?" Daniel asked them.

"Nowhere special. We just have to stop at a motel and talk about a few things. First off, this car is of no use to Dwight. Because as soon as word gets out that Chad is missing, the police will remember having stopped us. We may have to hang onto you overnight so you won't tell anyone about the van until it's long gone."

"What if I promised not to say anything?"

Phil laughed. "You've got to be kidding. You chase me all over the stadium to help your friend. Then you make me take you along because you think I'm a security man. You think all three of us are kidnapping Chad Whiteford. So you make a break for it and try to get the police involved. And now you tell me you're going to promise not to say anything? That's a good one, kid. A real good one."

"You don't have to call me kid, you know. My name's Daniel."

"Well, believe it or not, Daniel, it's nice to know you. I know you don't think much of me right now. But down deep I'm really a decent guy. I like people who are true to their friends and brave even when they shouldn't be. You see, the same thing that made you want to help your friend is the thing that makes me want to help his father. Loyalty."

Daniel felt a little sick. "I would have thought your reason was money." He almost wished he hadn't said it as soon as it was out of his mouth. "I care about Chad because he's my friend. Not because I'm being paid."

The smile faded from Phil Schaefer's face. "Yeah, well, we all gotta do what we all gotta do."

Daniel didn't understand that. All he cared about now was trying to convince these men that he could be trusted. Now that he knew Chad was with his father and that his father wouldn't hurt him, he was going to try again to get away and tell the police where they could find Chad.

The problem was, he was sitting in the front seat of a car with a man on either side of him. And, anyway, until they got together with Mr. Whiteford and Chad at the motel, Daniel didn't know where Chad was.

9

Meeting Mr. Whiteford

During the long trip out of the bustling city, Daniel prayed that Mr. Kaufman would quickly figure out the whole situation. There was probably no way for him to know that the kidnapper was Chad's father. But maybe that idea would come to Mrs. Whiteford when she heard the news.

Daniel felt sorry for Mr. Kaufman. He was sure Kenny would rather do anything than call someone's parents and tell them their boy was missing. And that a mysterious man had been nosing around and leaving false messages.

For the first time, Daniel thought of what his own parents would think when they heard *he* was missing. It almost made him cry. He knew somehow that he was going to be safe. No one here was the type who would hurt a kid. But his parents couldn't know that.

Just the same, he was still scared. How long would they keep him? And then where would they leave him? They knew he could send the police after them fairly quickly with what he knew. So he figured they would probably try to leave him somewhere where he couldn't do them any harm for a while.

He hoped that didn't mean they were going to tie him up or leave him in the middle of some forest where he couldn't find a phone or anyone to help. He had already surprised himself by acting so bravely. But he sure didn't want to be left alone somewhere.

It was getting dark when they pulled off the road and into the parking lot of a tacky little motel called the Green Dragon. They drove to the back of the place. Now the car couldn't be seen from the street.

The van was parked in an alley behind the building also.

Inside a room near the back of the motel were Chad Whiteford and his father. Mr. Whiteford was a stocky man with short, black hair and a dark complexion. Chad sat idly looking at the Raiders' game program for that day.

"Look what my dad bought me," he told Daniel. "Mom didn't give me enough money for food and a program. But I got one anyway."

Daniel tried to smile. He wondered if Chad really knew what was going on. Chad looked as if there was nothing wrong at all.

Mr. Whiteford smiled and reached out to shake Daniel's hand. "So, you're Chad's friend," he said, his brown eyes twinkling. "Isn't it nice that Chad's mother asked me to pick him up at the game and take him for a few days?"

Daniel didn't shake Mr. Whiteford's hand. "Is that what you told Chad?" he asked.

"Of course," Mr. Whiteford said, his smile fading. "I always tell him only the truth."

"Then who did you tell him these two men were?"

"Business partners, which is what they are. What's troubling you, son?"

Mr. Whiteford asked the question with a threatening tone in his voice. He seemed to want Daniel to be quiet in front of Chad. But Daniel didn't want to be. If this man was going to kidnap his own son, at least Chad had a right to know what was going on.

"And what did you tell him about why Mr. Kaufman wasn't told that you were taking him?"

"I talked to Mr. Kaufman. At least Phil did. Right, Phil?"

"Sure I did. Chad, you remember my coming by earlier and asking for him, don't you?"

Chad nodded.

"You never talked to Mr. Kaufman. On my way back to find Chad, I saw him. He knew that Chad and I got separated."

"I must have seen him after you did then," Phil said.

"Impossible," Daniel said. "As soon as I left Mr. Kaufman I spotted Chad and his father going one way and you coming the other. If you guys are going to kidnap somebody, you ought to at least tell him that's what you're doing."

Mr. Whiteford glared at him. "Kidnap? Why would I have to kidnap my own son?"

"Because you're not supposed to be seeing him except at his mother's house. If you had permission to see him at the ball game, why did you have to run off with him before it was over?"

Mr. Whiteford changed the subject. "I just called his mother and let her know that I located him all right. And I told her where we'll be."

Daniel was surprised. "Did he, Chad?"

"Well, sort of."

"Then you won't mind if I call my parents so they'll know I'm all right? By now Mr. Kaufman has called them to tell them that Chad and I are missing."

Mr. Whiteford glanced around nervously. "Yeah, sure. That would be OK, I guess. I wouldn't say anything about the van or where we're staying, though, because we won't be here long. I have to return the van to the rental place."

Daniel wanted to shout, to convince Chad of what was really going on. But he wanted to call his parents while he had the chance. He knew if he shouted or said anything to get Mr. Whiteford more upset, he might be in real trouble.

He carefully dialed his home number, area code and all.

Mr. Whiteford, Phil Schaefer, and Stan Davis watched. While it was ringing, Mr. Whiteford told him, "You've got about a minute."

Daniel's mother answered.

"Hi, Mom! This is Daniel."

"Daniel! Did they find you? Where are you? Are you all right?"

"Sure, Mom. I'm fine. I'm with Chad Whiteford and his father. We left the ball game early. But they'll get me back to Mr. Kaufman in time to go home with the other guys."

"Well, what's going on, Daniel? Mr. Kaufman called the pastor and said you and Chad were missing. Why didn't you tell him where you were going?"

"I'll tell you all about it when I get home, Mom. I just wanted to let you know I was fine in case Mr. Kaufman called or anything."

"Daniel! Of course he called. And I want you to know how much fear you've put us through by not telling anyone where you were going. Can you imagine what went through our minds?"

"I know, Mom. And I'm sorry. I'll tell you all about it when I get home. I was hoping Dad and Jim and I could play that game Mr. Kaufman told us about last Sunday."

"Game? What game?"

"Dad and Jim will remember. The one we heard about last Sunday night." Mr. Whiteford was signaling for Daniel to finish the call. "I have to go now, Mom. Don't worry about Chad and me. We're with Mr. Whiteford."

"But, Daniel, we don't even know Mr. Whiteford, and—"

"Bye, Mom."

"That was a good job, kid," Mr. Whiteford said, but he wasn't smiling. "Now that your mom and Chad's mom both know you're with me, we can talk frankly to each other, can't we?"

"You don't have to talk frankly with me, Mr. Whiteford. I know what this is all about. It's Chad who has a right to know. I mean, I was right, wasn't I? Chad's mother didn't know anything about this. And it's not legal, is it? It's against the law. You're not supposed to be seeing him. And I know you're not supposed to be taking him away."

Chad sat on the edge of the bed, looking puzzled and worried. His father sat next to him and put his arm around him, but Chad was stiff. "Is it true, Dad? Didn't Mom know? Is that why you carried me out of the stadium? Is that why you ran, pretending we were just having fun?"

Mr. Whiteford nodded slowly. "I didn't want your friends or Mr. Kaufman to see you. We waited until you got separated from Daniel. Whoever was closest to you at that point was supposed to grab you and run."

"But if anyone else had grabbed me, I would have screamed and cried."

"I know. We were lucky. It would have been very difficult if I hadn't been close by when you and Daniel got caught in the crowd. But now that we're together, I want you to come and live with me. I have a new job in another town. And I have a nice apartment."

"No, Dad! I don't want to make you feel bad. But I don't want to live with you. I want to stay with Mom. If you'd come back there and live with us, we could all be together again."

Mr. Whiteford stood and paced the room. To Daniel it appeared that he was almost ready to cry. "Chad, that's what I want, too. But your mother just won't have it. She makes up stories about me, tells lies about me, won't let me see you. She even said I couldn't come to see you at all anymore."

"She did?"

"Yes!"

"Are you sure? I never heard her say that. She told me you were coming again next month."

"See? See what she does? It isn't true. She tells you I'm coming. Then she tells me I can't come. Then when I don't show up, she tells you that I must not care about you."

"She's never done that."

"But she will. Because that's the kind of person she is. She lies."

"She does not, Dad! I've never heard her lie! She's never lied to me!"

Mr. Whiteford stood next to Chad, who had begun to cry. "Are you sure she's never lied to you, Chad? Hasn't she ever told you why we got a divorce?"

"No! She said someday I would know. She just said you two had a lot of problems and couldn't work them out. She never said it was only your fault."

Mr. Whiteford didn't seem to know what to say.

"She always told me it was my fault," he said.

"Well, then maybe that's what she thinks. But she didn't tell me that. Dad, you don't have to take me away. She'll let you see me!"

"But I don't want to see you only every month or so. I want you to stay with me, to live in my place, to let me buy you things and take you to school, to have dinner with you every night. I want you to really be my son."

"I am your son, Dad. But what you're doing now is going to hurt Mom bad. Real bad."

10
Escape Attempt

Chad Whiteford's father grew more and more agitated over the next hour as his son argued with him. Chad didn't want to go anywhere with his father. He wanted to be returned to the ballpark so that he could ride back home with his friends.

"It's a little too late for that now," his father said angrily. "Your mother already knows I have you. So does Daniel's mother. That means everyone in that church of yours knows, too, and is praying for you and probably against me right now."

Daniel decided to speak for the first time in more than an hour. "That also means that Mr. Kaufman knows. And you know what that means."

Mr. Whiteford stared at Daniel as if he wished Phil Schaefer had never decided to bring him along. "No, what does that mean, Mr. Know-It-All?"

"It means that Raider security and the local police know about it, too."

Phil Schaefer and Stan Davis, who had been sitting in a corner by themselves, chatting quietly during the whole argument, looked at each other, then at Mr. Whiteford. "If an all-points bulletin has gone out on the boys, Dwight, the cops who stopped us know they had Daniel in their hands for a few minutes and let him get away."

"Yeah, but how will they find us? You gotta admit this place is like a million other two-bit motels in this town."

Phil shrugged and shook his head. "You never know. They have the description and license on the wagon. So we're gonna have a tough time returning that to the rental place."

"Why, Phil? Didn't you rent that under a phony name?"

"No, I didn't. I didn't think I'd need to. The plan was to take Chad in the van. We didn't count on lifting two kids, you know. In fact, Dwight, if what Chad is saying is true, we're not real happy about having involved ourselves in this little caper."

"What do you mean? You're in this as deep as I am. From what you tell me, you lied to the police. And you've been with me all the way."

"That was because we believed you, Dwight. And we believed that sometimes a person has to break the law to do the right thing. If your kid was being abused by a mother who lied to you and to him and who wouldn't let you come to see him, well—"

"That's one thing," Stan Davis chimed in. "But this, if it's true . . . if you're the liar and Chad would rather stay with his mother, why—"

"So, are you guys bailing out on me, or what? Remember the second half of your payment is due when Chad is home safely with me. And not before that."

Phil and Stan glanced briefly at each other. "We're still in," Phil said miserably. "But we don't like it."

"So, what are you going to do, cry about it? You'd better ditch that station wagon somewhere. And when you do, bring us back something to eat."

Chad turned on the radio to see how the Raiders had done. During the few moments before the sports news, they heard: "A young boy and his friend were abducted from

Raider Stadium today, apparently by the boy's estranged father. Names of the boys are being withheld. But authorities believe the boys and the father, along with at least one accomplice, remain at large in the greater metropolitan area."

Later they heard that the Raiders had lost four to three in ten innings.

Phil Schaefer told Dwight Whiteford he thought it would be better to leave the station wagon right where it was, out of sight in the alley behind the motel. "And we should probably stay put right here until morning, too."

"Yeah, but what are we going to do with the other kid? He told his mother he would be back at the stadium in time to go home with rest of the group."

"Yeah," Daniel said. "They're waiting for me. I'm sure Mr. Kaufman would have heard from my mom. And by now she knows the whole story."

"Which is a good reason not to let you go so quickly," Mr. Whiteford said. "Not that I wouldn't love to. You've been a real pain. But you would be able to give them a pretty good idea where we are."

"But if I'm not back there soon, you're guilty of kidnapping me, aren't you?"

"I don't know," Mr. Whiteford said. "What if I am? What difference does it make anymore?"

Just thinking that way made him angry. He ripped a painting off the wall and flung it across the room. Then he grabbed the phone.

Phil Schaefer dived across the bed and wrestled it from his hands, nearly knocking Chad to the floor.

"I know you're frustrated, Dwight. But we need that phone. We may have to order food to be delivered."

"Are you kidding? By now there are pictures of me and the kids all over the television news. Forget it. We can't risk it. Now you and Stan get out and get us something. A pizza. Anything."

"Can you handle both kids yourself, Dwight?"

"Ha! I'll just plant myself by the only door and expect

you guys to get back before I fall asleep. Now, get going! I'm hungry."

There was an Atlanta Braves baseball game on television. Mr. Whiteford told the boys they could watch that if they were quiet and left him alone.

"Daniel, I'm scared," Chad said quietly as they lay next to each other on the floor, chins in their hands, elbows propped up.

"Me, too," Daniel said. "But I don't think your dad would hurt you, do you?"

"I don't know. He doesn't seem to be making any sense. I can't tell if he really loves me and misses me, or if he's just trying to hurt my mom by taking me away. Who's going to take care of me when he's working? Where will I sleep? Who will my friends be? Where will I go to school? He doesn't go to church, so I don't guess I'll get to go either."

"Yes, you will, Chad," Daniel whispered. "You're going to get out of this. There's no way your dad will be able to take care of you and hide you from the police and your mother and everyone else. He'd have to change his name and even his looks, because everyone will see his picture."

"Why would they see his picture?"

"Your mom would give it to the newspapers. That is, if she wants you back and you know she does."

"I know. But how will anyone find me?"

"I don't know. But I'll be praying about it." Mr. Whiteford seemed suspicious of their whispering. "Just be quiet and watch the game," he said. He knelt on the floor near Chad and said, "You know I'm only doing this because I love you, don't you?"

Chad didn't say anything. He didn't even look at his father.

"Well, don't you?" his father insisted. Chad shrugged.

"Well, you can believe it, because it's true."

Chad turned to look at him. "If you really loved me, you'd let me stay home with Mom. That's the best thing for me."

It was so true and such a clear way to say it that Daniel looked over at Mr. Whiteford, almost as if he was going to speak up and agree. He knew that would be wrong, that it would just make Mr. Whiteford angry again. So he didn't say anything.

Dwight Whiteford slowly got to his feet and moved toward the window next to the door. He pulled the curtain aside just a bit and stared out into the darkness. From behind, Daniel thought he looked tired. And sad.

Daniel couldn't tell, but it looked as though Mr. Whiteford might have been crying. Daniel held a finger up to his lips to silently instruct Chad to be quiet. He slipped to his feet and tiptoed up behind Chad's father.

If he could only race for the door, pull the chain off, turn the lock, then the handle, and run through the parking lot to the street. He could stop in at the registration desk and scream for help. Or he could just try to outrun Mr. Whiteford and get to a phone somewhere.

He didn't think Mr. Whiteford would chase him and risk leaving Chad by himself. Daniel hoped that if Mr. Whiteford did chase him, Chad would know enough to get away or phone someone.

As Daniel got close to Mr. Whiteford, he could see that he was crying. Any second he would have to wipe his eyes with a handkerchief or his hand or something. At that instant, Daniel decided, he would leap for the door.

Sure enough, in less than a minute, Mr. Whiteford pulled a kerchief from his pocket and dabbed at his eyes. Daniel charged to the door, popped the chain off, turned the lock, and turned the handle.

The door flew open. The cool night air rushed in as Daniel sprinted out. He was into his third full-speed step when his feet left the ground.

Chad's father had grabbed him by the collar and the belt. Then he slung him into the room where he bounced on the bed and rolled off to the floor. He thought about pretending he had been hurt bad, giving Chad a chance to run out. But there was no time.

Mr. Whiteford hurried over to him. "I'm sorry I had to do that. But you've got to know I can't let you go running off like that. No way. You're too valuable to me right now. You know too much."

Daniel felt like crying. He wasn't hurt. But being grabbed in midair like that had shocked him. For a second he thought he'd caught Dwight Whiteford off guard. He really thought he was free.

And now he and Chad were less free than ever.

11
The Threat

"Dad!" Chad shouted. "You could have hurt him."

"He shouldn't have tried to get away," Mr. Whiteford said.

"He was only trying to help me," Chad wailed, crying now. "Just like he has all day long. He spent time with me on the bus. He sat with me at the game. He was my buddy at the stadium. He chased us when he thought you were kidnapping me—which you were, only I didn't know it."

Mr. Whiteford's shoulders sagged. He sat heavily in a chair by the door.

"How can you say that, Chad? I'm risking everything today, just so I can take you with me."

"You're risking everything, all right," Chad said, "You're breaking the law. You're hurting Mom. And you don't even care what I think. I don't have any say in all this."

Daniel was proud of Chad for speaking up. He had been afraid Chad would be too timid to really say what he thought.

"You have a say in this," Mr. Whiteford said. "You tell me you don't want to live with me—that you'd rather live with your mother—that you'd like to see me go to jail for kidnapping my own son—and I'll turn myself in right now."

Chad looked stunned. "You will?"

"Absolutely. I'll call the police right now to come and get you and Daniel. But I warn you, I'd rather be dead than to see that happen."

"What do you mean?"

"What do you think I mean, Chad?"

"That you'd kill yourself?"

"Figure it out for yourself."

"Well, Dad, what I want is just what you said except for the last part. I want to go home. I want to live with Mom. But I don't want to see you go to jail, and there's no way I want to see you kill yourself."

"I couldn't live in jail, Chad."

"I don't think they'd make you go to jail if you called Mom right now and let me go home."

"I don't think I could live with that either, Chad."

"Well, I can't fix everything, Dad. What am I supposed to do?"

Mr. Whiteford buried his head in his hands. "You're supposed to want to live with me the most. More than with your mother. More than anything in the world."

"But I don't."

"I know! I know! But why? Why not?"

"I'm just happier there, that's all. And if you can't come home to live with Mom and Marie and me, then I want you to visit whenever you can."

"But when I come to see you, your mother wants me to spend time with Marie, too."

"What's wrong with that, Dad? She's your little girl."

"But I hardly knew her. And I didn't want a daughter. I wanted another son."

Chad shook his head and folded his arms. "I don't understand you, Dad. I don't understand you at all."

A knock at the door made Mr. Whiteford jump from his chair. He peeked through the curtain. He opened the door for

Phil Schaefer and Stan Davis, who were carrying pizzas. "All clear out there?" Mr. Whiteford asked.

They nodded.

"No problems?"

"Nope. Just a long wait for the pizzas."

"I'm starved," he said. He tore into a box and began eating before anyone else.

The three men ate quickly. Mr. Whiteford finally noticed that neither of the boys were eating at all. "Here!" he said with his mouth full, pointing to the pizza. "Have some! Come on!"

Chad shook his head. "I don't feel like eating," he said.

"You have to eat something!"

"I don't either! I'm not hungry! Leave me alone!"

That embarrassed Mr. Whiteford. Maybe he hadn't realized before that his son had a temper something like his. He turned his attention to Daniel. "How about you?"

"Got stuffed at the ball game," he said. "Anyway, I guess I'm kind of nervous."

Mr. Whiteford laughed. "Guess I can't blame you."

"What are you going to do?" Daniel asked.

No one spoke. It seemed to Daniel it was a logical question. He simply wanted to know what was going to happen to himself and Chad. He figured Mr. Whiteford had made up his mind to keep Chad, even against Chad's own wishes. But he also figured that he himself was in the way. They would decide where to dump him, so that he couldn't tell anyone where they were until they were long gone. He'd be stuck out in the middle of nowhere.

"I don't know yet," Mr. Whiteford said. "I guess if Chad doesn't want to come and live with me, I'll just let both of you go and see if you can find your way back home."

"Dad!" Chad scolded. "You'd really do that?"

"Course not! I don't know what I'm gonna do yet. But somehow I have to convince you you'd be better off with me than with your mother."

"Never," Chad whispered under his breath.

"What? What'd you say?"

"I said never," Chad said loud and clear.

His father jumped from his chair and kicked an end table. That sent the telephone crashing to the floor and the receiver flying off the hook. In his rage he grabbed the phone and yanked it hard, nearly pulling it from the wall. The wires stretched. But when they didn't break free, he grunted and whined and gave another huge tug. He finally freed the phone from the wall.

His face was flushed with anger. His eyes were black and menacing. Even Phil Schaefer and Stan Davis stood and moved away from him. He seemed to be looking for somewhere to throw the heavy phone.

When he took aim at the window, Phil and Stan rushed toward him. But they were too late. The phone flew through the curtains and smashed the glass. It bounced out into the parking lot.

"Oh, great," Phil said. "Now you've done it. If you don't think that's not going to bring the manager running, you're out of your mind. If you can't control yourself any better than this, I have to think the boy *is* better off with his mother."

"Just try and take him," Dwight Whiteford challenged. But before anyone could respond, a loud knock at the door silenced them.

Mr. Whiteford pulled a hundred dollar bill from his wallet and handed it to Phil, nodding toward the door and whispering, "Just tell him we were playing around and got carried away. Offer him the hundred and tell him we'll calm down."

Phil popped the chain, turned the lock, and opened the door. But rather than the manager, he saw three uniformed policemen and a detective, guns drawn and barking orders.

"Up against the wall, feet back, and spread them." While the uniformed officers were searching the three men, the detective asked the boys if they were Chad Whiteford and Daniel Bradford. They nodded. He turned back to the men.

"Which of you is Dwight Whiteford?"

Chad's dad didn't say anything, but Phil and Stan both nodded toward him. The detective said, "You're under arrest on two counts of aggravated kidnapping. You have the right to remain silent. Anything you say may be used against you in a court of law. If you cannot afford an attorney, one will be provided for you. Do you understand these rights as I have read them?"

Mr. Whiteford nodded.

"Do you wish to have an attorney present before you speak?"

He nodded again and was led out to a squad car.

"Tell me this," Phil Schaefer said. "How'd you find us so quickly?"

"You can thank young Mr. Bradford for that," the detective said. "When you were stopped in traffic earlier, one of our men thought he sensed something wrong. Everything checked out except for the way Daniel Bradford acted. And one thing he said. He told our officer that he hated to leave the game when the Raiders were leading. Our guy was listening to the game later when the Raiders tied it. He learned they had trailed since the Cubs first scored in the second.

"So, he figured Daniel was trying to tell him something. Apparently he was."

"But how did you find us here?" Davis asked.

"Daniel Bradford again. Just about the time our man discovered that Daniel was trying to tell him something, the all-points bulletin was announced, complete with descriptions. The officer called in his hunch that he had already seen Daniel. He was told that both mothers had been contacted, and that one of the boys had obviously been trying to send a message through a clue. You want to tell them about it yourself, Daniel?"

Daniel was so relieved that the police were there, and that he and Chad would be getting home safely that night. He almost didn't hear the questions. "Oh yeah, sure. I told my mother I wanted to get home in time to play the game we had heard about in church last Sunday night."

"Yeah, so?"

"Well, the only game we heard about last Sunday night was a witchcraft-type thing called the Bad Dragons. Mr. Kaufman warned everyone about it. Mom knew I wouldn't really want to play that game. So she must have told the police what I said."

"That's right," the detective said. "It took us a while to put it all together. But we checked out every establishment that had dragon in its name. And we discovered the station wagon here. Thanks to a big coincidence, Daniel, we found you."

Daniel smiled. He knew it was more than coincidence.

Moody Press, a ministry of the Moody Bible Institute,
is designed for education, evangelization, and edification.
If we may assist you in knowing more about Christ
and the Christian life, please write us without obligation:
Moody Press, c/o MLM, Chicago, Illinois 60610